There Are No Guilty People

The Death Penalty, Moral Conscience, and the Illusion of Justice

A Modern Translation

Adapted for the Contemporary Reader

Leo Tolstoy

Translated by Tim Zengerink

Table of Contents

Preface - Message to the Reader

What If You Could Help Rebuild the Greatest Library in Human History?

Thousands of years ago, the Library of Alexandria stood as the crown jewel of human achievement — a sanctuary where the collected wisdom of every known civilization was gathered, preserved, and shared freely.

And then, it was lost.

Through fire, conquest, and the slow erosion of time, humanity lost not just books — but ideas, dreams, discoveries, and stories that could have changed the world forever.

Today, the Library of Alexandria lives again — and you are invited to be a part of its restoration.

Our mission is simple yet profound:

To rebuild the greatest library the world has ever known, and to translate all timeless works into every language and dialect, so that no seeker of knowledge is ever left behind again.

By joining our movement to rebuild the modern Library of Alexandria, you become part of an unprecedented mission:

Unlimited Access to the Greatest Audiobooks & eBooks Ever Written:

Instantly explore thousands of legendary works—Plato, Shakespeare, Jane Austen, Leo Tolstoy, and countless more. All instantly available to read or listen, placing a complete literary universe at your fingertips.

Beautiful Paperback & Deluxe Editions at Printing Cost

Own any title as an elegant paperback, deluxe hardcover, or stunning collectible boxset—offered to you at true printing cost, delivered straight to your door. Build your personal Library of Alexandria, crafted for beauty, built for durability, and worthy of proud display.

Fresh Translations for Modern Readers—in Every Language & Dialect

Enjoy timeless masterpieces reimagined in clear, contemporary language—no more outdated phrases or obscure references. Alongside the original versions, we're tirelessly translating these classics into every language and dialect imaginable, ensuring accessibility and understanding across cultures and generations.

Join a Global Renaissance of Literature & Knowledge

You directly support expanding our library, publishing deluxe editions at true cost, translating works into all global languages, and bringing humanity's greatest stories to people everywhere. By joining today, you're not just preserving a legacy of masterpieces; you set in motion a powerful wave of literary accessibility.

Become a Torchbearer of Knowledge.

Join us for free now at **LibraryofAlexandria.com**

Together, we will ensure that the light of human wisdom never fades again.

With gratitude and a shared love of knowledge,

The Modern Library of Alexandria Team

Visit:

www.libraryofalexandria.com

Or scan the code below:

Introduction

The Ultimate Condemnation of the Death Penalty and the Machinery of Moral Judgment

Leo Tolstoy's There Are No Guilty People stands as one of the most impassioned, courageous, and morally uncompromising indictments of capital punishment in modern literature. Written in 1909, just a year before Tolstoy's death, this short but powerful essay and fictional fragment was a direct response to the state executions that continued under the Russian Tsarist regime. The work was so provocative that it was banned during Tolstoy's lifetime and widely suppressed. Yet its message resounds louder than ever today, speaking across generations and borders to challenge the moral foundations of state-sanctioned justice.

Tolstoy, by this point in his life, had fully embraced a form of Christian anarchism—rejecting all violence, authority, coercion, and institutional religion in favor of radical nonviolence, ethical purity, and universal compassion. There Are No Guilty People is both an expression of that philosophy and a polemical text aimed at awakening the conscience of its readers. Unlike his earlier fiction, which often couches moral themes in rich character studies and narrative arcs, this work is raw, direct, and unflinching. It combines the rhetorical force of a public appeal with the philosophical clarity of a moral manifesto.

In its central argument, Tolstoy declares that the judicial and penal systems—especially when they culminate in execution—are not instruments of justice, but tools of cruelty and dehumanization. He dismantles the very concept of guilt, arguing that human beings are shaped by social, economic, and historical forces beyond their control, and that no person can be condemned without also indicting the society that shaped them. He suggests that by killing those it deems guilty, the state reveals not justice but its own moral bankruptcy. The act of execution, in Tolstoy's view, is not a punishment of evil—it is the performance of evil in the name of order.

This introduction explores the historical background, philosophical roots, and emotional power of There Are No Guilty People, placing it in the context of Tolstoy's lifelong resistance to violence and institutional hypocrisy. It considers how the text anticipates modern critiques of the prison-industrial complex, structural injustice, and the death penalty itself.

More than a historical document or literary curio, the work remains a powerful provocation, asking each reader to consider not only what justice is, but what it costs—and whom it serves.

A Voice Against the Gallows: Tolstoy's Moral Rebellion Against the State

To understand There Are No Guilty People, one must understand the Russia in which it was written. The early 20th century was a time of political repression, social unrest, and widespread state violence. The 1905 Russian Revolution had recently failed, and the government responded with a wave of executions targeting revolutionaries, dissenters, and even innocent people caught in the machinery of suspicion. It was in this atmosphere that Tolstoy, nearing the end of his life, felt compelled to speak with unflinching urgency.

Tolstoy's condemnation of the death penalty was not new. He had long rejected violence in all forms, inspired by the teachings of Jesus, particularly the Sermon on the Mount. What distinguishes this work, however, is its intensity and rhetorical clarity. He does not merely argue against the death penalty on utilitarian or political grounds—he condemns it as a moral abomination. To execute another human being, he argues, is to act as God while possessing none of God's mercy or omniscience. It is to arrogate to oneself the right to judge, a right that no mortal possesses.

In the fictional portion of the work, Tolstoy presents the story of a man condemned to die for murder. The portrait is not of a monster, but of a deeply human figure: flawed, broken, and shaped by circumstances beyond his choosing. The point is not to excuse his actions, but to understand them—and in understanding, to see that justice cannot be delivered through violence. Tolstoy forces the reader to feel the dread, confusion, and abandonment of the condemned man, who, in his final hours, grapples with the meaning of his life and death.

But Tolstoy's message goes deeper. He argues that the very concept of guilt is a societal fiction. Humans are not inherently good or evil; they are molded by conditions—poverty, ignorance, injustice, fear. A murderer, he says, is not born but made. And if we are to condemn him, we must also condemn ourselves: for creating the conditions in which violence becomes inevitable, and then disowning our complicity by calling it justice.

In this light, the story becomes a mirror. The reader is not asked to condemn or forgive, but to reflect. What gives us the right to punish? What lies behind our desire for retribution? What would justice look like if it were rooted in love rather than fear?

This modern translation of There Are No Guilty People aims to preserve the precision, passion, and moral clarity of Tolstoy's original while making the language accessible to contemporary audiences. Every effort has been made to retain the emotional force of the narrative and the rhetorical rhythm of Tolstoy's appeal to the human conscience.

In conclusion, There Are No Guilty People is not merely a plea against the death penalty. It is a confrontation with the entire idea of punishment, hierarchy, and human judgment. It invites the reader to step outside the courtroom and into the soul; to ask whether justice built on fear can ever produce peace; and to consider the possibility that redemption lies not in execution, but in understanding, compassion, and transformation. Tolstoy's voice, unbending and luminous, reminds us that until we see all people as our brothers and sisters, we will never escape the shadow of the gallows. His words are not an argument—they are a cry from the heart of humanity.

Chapter I

My situation is both strange and difficult to understand. There are probably no beggars, suffering under the wealth and power of the rich, who feel the same deep anger and pain that I do. I see the injustice, cruelty, and disrespect that the wealthy show toward the poor. I also feel the terrible struggles and humiliation of workers— the real creators of everything that makes life possible. I have felt this for a long time, and as the years have passed, my feelings have only grown stronger. Now, they are almost unbearable.

Even though I see this injustice so clearly, I still live among the rich, surrounded by their selfishness and waste. And no matter how much I want to, I cannot leave. I don't have the knowledge or the strength to change my life in a way that would allow me to meet my basic needs—food, sleep, clothing, and transportation—without feeling ashamed.

There was a time when I tried to change my situation. I wanted to live in a way that matched my beliefs. But my past, my family, and my responsibilities made it impossible to escape. Or maybe I just didn't know how. I wasn't strong enough.

Now, I am over eighty years old and growing weaker. I no longer try to free myself. But strangely, as I become physically weaker, my awareness of how wrong my position is only grows stronger, making my life even harder to bear.

It has occurred to me that maybe I am in this position for a reason. Perhaps I am meant to speak the truth about what I feel, to expose the injustice that causes my suffering. Maybe by doing so, I can help open the eyes of those who still don't see the truth. If even a few people begin to understand, perhaps the suffering of the poor will be eased.

Maybe the fact that I am in this position gives me a unique chance to expose the fake and unfair relationships between people. I can tell the full truth about it, without trying to defend myself. I don't want to make excuses for my life, and I have no reason to envy the rich or encourage resentment among the poor.

I find myself filled with shame and disgust for the privileged class I live among, yet I cannot separate myself from them. Still, I must be careful not to make the mistake that many reformers make—ignoring the flaws of the poor while blaming the wealthy for everything. The mistakes of past generations have created this system, and while that does not excuse the wealthy, it does make the problem more complicated.

Because I don't feel the need to defend myself, and because I do not fear the power of an awakened people, I am in a rare position to see and speak the truth. Maybe this is why life has placed me here. And if that is the case, then I must do my best to make use of it.

Chapter II

Alexander Ivanovich Volgin was a single man who worked as a bank clerk in Moscow, making eight thousand roubles a year. He was well-liked and respected among his friends. He was visiting a country estate owned by a rich landowner who was married to his cousin.

After an evening spent playing cards for small bets with the family, Volgin went to his room feeling tired. He placed his watch, silver cigarette case, wallet, leather coin purse, and a small pocket brush and comb on a side table covered with a white cloth. Then, he took off his clothes—his coat, vest, shirt, pants, underwear, silk socks, and English-made boots. He put on his nightshirt and robe. His watch showed that it was midnight.

Lying on his stomach, he smoked a cigarette and thought about the day for a few minutes. Then, he blew out the candle, turned onto his side, and finally fell asleep around one o'clock, though he had trouble settling down.

The next morning, he woke up at eight, put on his slippers and robe, and rang the bell.

The old butler, Stephen, who had served the family for thirty years and had six grandchildren, hurried into the room. He carried Volgin's freshly polished boots, a well-brushed suit, and a clean shirt. Volgin thanked him and asked about the weather, as the blinds were kept closed so guests could sleep as late as they wanted, even until eleven. He also asked if his hosts had slept well.

Seeing that it was still early, he began his morning routine. The washstand and dressing table were neatly arranged with everything he needed—soap, toothbrush, hairbrush, nail scissors, and a file. He washed his face and hands carefully, trimmed and cleaned his nails, and wiped away any loose skin with a towel. Then, he sponged his body from head to toe.

Standing in front of the mirror, he brushed his curly beard, which was starting to turn gray, with two English-made brushes, parting it down the middle. Then, he combed his thinning hair with a large tortoiseshell comb.

After dressing—putting on his undershirt, socks, boots, pants with elegant suspenders, and vest—he sat in a comfortable chair without his coat. He lit a cigarette and relaxed, thinking about where he should take his morning walk. Should he go to the park or to the wooded area called Littleports? The name always made him smile. He decided on Littleports.

He also needed to reply to Simon Nicholaevich's letter, but there was plenty of time for that.

Glancing at his watch, he saw it was nearly nine o'clock. He put the watch in his vest pocket, his purse—holding the remaining money from the 180 roubles he had brought for the trip—in his pants pocket, and his cigarette case and lighter in another. He slipped two clean handkerchiefs into his coat pockets and left the room, as usual leaving a mess for Stephen to clean up. Stephen, now over fifty, was used to this and expected a small tip for his work.

Before leaving, Volgin glanced at himself in a mirror. Satisfied with his appearance, he headed to the dining room.

Breakfast had already been set out by the housekeeper, the footman, and the assistant butler, who had woken up early to sharpen his son's scythe before coming to work. A gleaming silver samovar filled with boiling water stood on the table, along with a coffee pot, hot milk, cream, butter, and a variety of fancy breads and biscuits.

Only three other people were at the table—the host's second son, his tutor (a student), and the secretary. The head of the household, an active member of the local government and a dedicated farmer, had already left for work at eight.

As Volgin drank his coffee, he chatted with the student and secretary about the weather and last night's card game. They also discussed Theodorite's rude behavior toward his father the night before.

Theodorite, the eldest son of the family, was a troublemaker. His real name was Theodore, but someone had once jokingly called him Theodorite, and the name had stuck. He had gone to university but dropped out in his second year. Then, he joined a cavalry regiment but left that as well. Now, he did nothing except complain and criticize everything around him.

Meanwhile, the rest of the household was still asleep—Anna Mikhailovna, the lady of the house; her sister, a general's widow; and a landscape painter who lived with them.

After breakfast, Volgin picked up his expensive panama hat from the hallway table—it had cost twenty roubles—and grabbed his walking cane with its carved ivory handle.

Stepping out onto the veranda, he admired the flowers in the garden. In the center was a round flower bed with red, white, and blue flowers arranged in rings. The initials of the mistress of the house were spelled out in the middle with carefully planted greenery.

He walked past the flower garden into an avenue lined with ancient lime trees, where peasant girls were sweeping with spades and brooms. The gardener was measuring something, and a young boy was pulling a cart.

After passing them, Volgin entered the vast park, which stretched over 125 acres, filled with old trees and crisscrossed by well-maintained paths.

As he walked along his favorite path, passing the summer house and heading toward the open fields, he enjoyed the fresh air. The park was lovely, but the fields beyond were even more beautiful.

To the right, women digging up potatoes created a bright splash of red and white against the green fields. To the left, golden wheat fields, rolling meadows, and grazing cattle stretched toward the horizon. In the distance, just off to the right, stood the dark, towering oak trees of Littleports.

Volgin took a deep breath and felt completely relaxed. He was thankful for this quiet getaway at his cousin's estate, a much-needed break from his busy job at the bank.

"People who live in the countryside are lucky," Volgin thought. "Of course, with all his farming and local government work, the owner of this estate doesn't have much free time, but that's his problem."

Volgin shook his head, lit another cigarette, and walked forward confidently in his sturdy English boots. His thoughts drifted to the heavy workload waiting for him in the winter at the bank. "I'll be there every day from ten to two, sometimes even until five. Then there are the board meetings... and private meetings with clients... and the Duma. But here... it's wonderful. Maybe a little boring, but not for long." He smiled to himself.

After wandering through Littleports, he decided to take a shortcut across a plowed field. A herd of cows, calves, sheep, and pigs from the nearby village was grazing there. The shortest way back to the park was through the animals. As he walked, the sheep ran off one by one, followed by the pigs. Two small piglets, however, stood still and stared at him with serious expressions.

The shepherd boy called after the sheep and cracked his whip.

"We're so far behind Europe," Volgin thought, remembering his frequent vacations abroad. "You wouldn't see a single cow like that anywhere over there."

Curious about the path splitting off from his own and the owner of the herd, he called out to the boy.

"Whose herd is this?"

The boy, staring in awe at Volgin's fine hat, neatly groomed beard, and, most of all, his gold-rimmed glasses, was too startled to answer right away. When Volgin repeated the question, the boy finally snapped out of it.

"Ours."

"But whose is 'ours'?" Volgin asked, smiling and shaking his head.

The boy was dressed in worn-out clothes. His shoes were made of woven birch bark, his legs were wrapped in linen bands, and his dirty, ragged shirt had a tear at the shoulder. His cap was missing its peak.

"The Pirogov village herd," the boy finally answered.

"How old are you?"

"I don't know."

"Can you read?"

"No."

"Didn't you go to school?"

"Yes."

"But you didn't learn to read?"

"No."

"Where does that path lead?"

The boy told him, and Volgin continued walking toward the house, already thinking about how he would tease Nicholas Petrovich about the poor state of the village schools, despite all his supposed efforts to improve them.

As he neared the house, Volgin checked his watch and realized it was already past eleven. He remembered that Nicholas Petrovich was planning to drive into town, and he had meant to give him a letter to mail to Moscow. But he hadn't written it yet. The letter was important— it was for a friend, asking him to bid on a painting of the Madonna at an upcoming auction.

When he reached the house, he saw a carriage parked by the front door. Four strong, well-fed, well-groomed horses were harnessed to it. The black lacquer on the carriage gleamed in the sunlight. The coachman sat up straight on the driver's seat, wearing a kaftan with a silver belt. The horses occasionally shook their heads, making the silver bells on their harnesses jingle softly.

At the entrance, a barefooted peasant in a ragged kaftan stood, his head uncovered. He bowed to Volgin.

"What do you need?" Volgin asked.

"I came to see Nicholas Petrovich."

"Why?"

"I'm in trouble… my horse died," the man said.

Volgin started asking the peasant questions. The man explained his situation—he had five children, and the horse that had just died was his only one. Now, without it, he didn't know how he would survive. Tears filled his eyes.

"What will you do now?" Volgin asked.

"I'll have to beg," the man replied. Then, he dropped to his knees and refused to get up, no matter how much Volgin tried to stop him.

"What's your name?"

"Mitri Sudarikov," the peasant answered, still kneeling.

Volgin took three roubles from his wallet and gave them to the man. The peasant, grateful, bowed so low that his forehead touched the ground. Then, Volgin turned away and walked into the house, where his host was already waiting in the hallway.

"Where's your letter?" his host asked as he approached. "I'm about to leave."

"I'm really sorry! I'll write it right now if you can wait. I completely forgot. It's so peaceful here—it's easy to forget everything."

"That's fine, but hurry up. The horses have been standing for fifteen minutes already, and the flies are biting like crazy." Then he turned to the coachman. "Can you wait a little longer, Arsenty?"

"Why not?" the coachman replied, though he was thinking to himself, Why do they always rush us to get the horses ready if they're not even prepared to leave? We worked so hard getting everything set up, just to stand here and let the flies eat us alive.

"I'll be quick, I promise," Volgin said, heading toward his room. But before going in, he turned back to ask about the peasant.

"Did you see that man outside?"

"Yes," his host replied. "He's a drunk, but still, he's struggling. Now, hurry up!"

Volgin quickly took out his writing case, got a pen, and wrote the letter. He also filled out a cheque for 180 roubles and sealed everything in an envelope before handing it to his host.

"Goodbye," Volgin said as his host rushed out the door.

Afterward, Volgin spent time reading newspapers until lunch. He only read Liberal papers—The Russian Gazette, Speech, and sometimes The Russian Word. But he refused to touch The New Times, which his host subscribed to.

As he flipped through the pages, he read about politics, news from the Tsar, updates on the President and government ministers, and decisions made in the Duma. He was just about to move on to news about the theater, science, crime, and a cholera outbreak when the lunch bell rang.

The meal was prepared with the help of more than ten servants, including cooks, kitchen maids, housekeepers, butlers, and gardeners. The dining table was set beautifully for eight people, decorated with silver water jugs, wine decanters, kvass, mineral water, cut-glass cups, and fine table linens. Two footmen moved quickly around the room, constantly bringing in dishes, serving food, and clearing plates.

The hostess talked nonstop about everything she had done, thought about, or said that day. She seemed convinced that all of her thoughts and actions were brilliant and that anyone who disagreed was simply foolish. Volgin knew that most of what she said was nonsense, but he didn't let it show. Instead, he politely kept the conversation going.

Theodorite, on the other hand, sat quietly, looking grumpy. The student at the table occasionally spoke to the general's widow, but otherwise, the meal was filled with uncomfortable silences.

Whenever the conversation died down, Theodorite would suddenly say something, but instead of helping, his comments made the mood even worse. The room would fall into an awkward silence.

At those moments, the hostess would call for a dish that hadn't been served yet, sending the footman running to the kitchen or the housekeeper. He would return quickly, but the atmosphere remained dull.

No one really felt like talking or eating, but they forced themselves to do both. And so, lunch dragged on.

The peasant asking for help because his horse had died was named Mitri Sudarikov. The day before he went to see the landowner, he had spent the entire day trying to handle the situation.

First, he went to find Sanin, the knacker, in a nearby village. Since Sanin wasn't home, Mitri waited until he returned and then bargained over the price of the horse's skin. By the time they finished, it was already noon.

Then, Mitri needed to borrow a horse to move his dead one to a field for burial, since burying animals near the village was not allowed. Adrian refused to lend his horse because he was busy harvesting potatoes, but another neighbor, Stephen, took pity on Mitri and agreed to help. Stephen even helped lift the dead horse into the cart.

Before leaving, Mitri removed the horseshoes from his horse's front legs and gave them to his wife. One was broken, but the other was still good.

The burial was difficult. The shovel he used was dull, and he struggled to dig the grave. While he was still working, the knacker arrived, took off the horse's skin, and then Mitri finished covering the body with dirt.

Exhausted, he went to Matrena's hut, where he drank half a bottle of vodka with Sanin to ease his sadness. Afterward, he went home, argued with his wife, and lay down in the hay to sleep. He didn't bother undressing and used his tattered coat as a blanket. His wife stayed inside with their four daughters, the youngest only five weeks old.

Mitri woke up before sunrise, as usual. The moment he opened his eyes, he groaned, remembering the events of the previous day—the way his horse had struggled before collapsing. Now, he was left with nothing but the money from selling the skin—four roubles and eighty kopeks.

Getting up, he wrapped linen bands around his legs and walked into the house. His wife was busy feeding the stove with straw, holding their baby in one arm while her other breast hung loose from her dirty nightshirt.

Mitri crossed himself three times toward the corner where their religious icons hung. Then, mumbling a few meaningless words he called prayers, he quickly recited the Trinity, the Virgin's name, the Creed, and the Lord's Prayer.

"Is there any water?" he asked.

"The girl went to fetch some. I made tea. Are you going to see the squire?"

"Yes, I should go."

The smoke from the stove made him cough. He grabbed a rag from the wooden bench and stepped outside.

Just then, his daughter returned carrying a pail of water. Mitri scooped some into his mouth, spit it onto his hands, then took another mouthful to rinse his face. He wiped himself with the rag, smoothed his curly hair with his fingers, and started walking away.

A girl, about ten years old and wearing nothing but a dirty shirt, ran up to him.

"Good morning, Uncle Mitri," she said. "You're supposed to come help with the thrashing."

"I'll come later," he replied. He knew this was a favor he owed to Kumushkir, a poor farmer like himself, who had helped him last week when he was using a horse-powered threshing machine for his own grain.

"Tell them I'll be there by lunchtime. I have to go to Ugrumi first."

Mitri went back into the hut, changed his worn-out birch-bark shoes, adjusted the linen wraps on his legs, and set off to see the squire.

After receiving three roubles from Volgin and another three from Nicholas Petrovich, he went home, handed the money to his wife, and then headed to his neighbor's farm.

The threshing machine was already running, and the driver was shouting at the horses pulling it. The thin animals moved in slow circles, straining against their harnesses. The driver kept calling to them in a steady voice, "Come on, my dears."

Nearby, women worked quickly—some untying bundles of wheat, others raking up the loose straw and grains, and a few gathering large armfuls of wheat to hand to the men feeding the machine.

The work was in full swing.

As Mitri passed through the vegetable garden, he saw a girl wearing only a long shirt, digging up potatoes and placing them into a basket.

"Where's your grandfather?" he asked.

"In the barn," she answered.

Mitri walked into the barn and got to work right away. The old man, who was eighty, knew about Mitri's troubles. He greeted him and stepped aside, letting Mitri take over feeding the machine.

Mitri took off his ragged coat, placed it near the fence, and threw himself into work, gathering wheat and tossing it into the thresher.

The job continued without a break until noon.

The roosters had crowed two or three times, but no one paid attention. It wasn't that they didn't believe the birds—it was just that the noise of the machine and the chatter of the workers drowned everything out.

Finally, the loud whistle of the squire's steam thresher, three miles away, signaled that it was time to stop.

At that moment, the farm owner stepped into the barn. Though he was also eighty, he still stood tall and straight.

"It's time for dinner," he said.

The workers quickly wrapped up the job. They cleared away the straw, separated the grain from the chaff, and stored it properly. Then, they all headed toward the house.

The small hut where they ate was blackened with smoke because the stove had no chimney. Still, it had been cleaned up, and benches were arranged around the table so that all nine workers could sit, along with the farm owners.

On the table were simple foods—bread, soup, boiled potatoes, and kvass.

An old one-armed beggar, with a bag over his shoulder and a crutch to help him walk, came in while they were eating.

"Peace to this house. I hope you enjoy your meal. Please, give me something in the name of Christ."

"God will take care of you," said the mistress, an older woman who was the master's daughter-in-law. "Please don't be upset with us."

An old man standing near the door spoke up. "Martha, give him some bread. How can you turn him away?"

"I'm just thinking if we'll have enough," Martha said hesitantly.

"That's not right, Martha. God wants us to help those in need. Give him a piece of bread."

Martha obeyed, and the beggar went on his way.

Afterward, the man in charge of the threshing machine stood up, said grace, thanked the hosts, and went to rest.

Mitri didn't rest. Instead, he hurried to the shop to buy some tobacco, craving a smoke. As he smoked, he talked with a man from Demensk, asking about the price of cattle. He already knew he would have to sell a cow to get by.

When he returned, the others had already started working again, and so the labor continued until evening.

Among these exhausted, overworked, and underfed people—who were being slowly worn down by hardship—there were those who still thought of themselves as Christians. Others believed they were so modern and educated that they no longer needed religion. Yet, despite their beliefs, their lives were made comfortable by the hard labor of these workers. Not only that, but they also depended on millions of factory workers who produced the samovars, silverware, carriages, and machines they used every day.

They lived in the middle of all this suffering, seeing it yet pretending not to. Many of them were not cruel at heart—old men, women, young people, mothers, and children—yet they ignored what was happening around them.

There was an old bachelor who owned thousands of acres. He had spent his life in comfort and luxury, never doing any real work. He read The New Times and couldn't understand why the government allowed Jewish students to attend universities.

Then there was his guest, a former governor and now a high-ranking senator with a big salary. He read the news with satisfaction when he saw that a group of lawyers supported bringing back the death penalty.

Even their political rival, N. P., who read a liberal newspaper, was outraged that the government allowed a group called the "Union of Russian Men" to exist.

Meanwhile, a kind and gentle mother sat reading a story to her little daughter about a dog named Fox, who had injured some rabbits.

And then there was the little girl herself.

On her walks, she often saw other children—barefoot, hungry, searching the ground for fallen green apples. But she never thought of them as children like herself. To her, they were just part of the scenery, no different from the trees or the roads.

Why was this?

Thank You for Reading

Dear Reader,

We hope this timeless classic has sparked your imagination and enriched your literary journey. Now that you've turned the final page, we want to share a vision for the future of reading—one where every classic you've ever wanted to explore is at your fingertips, in a format that best suits your life.

We'd like to invite you to gain immediate, unlimited digital & audiobook access to hundreds of the most treasured literary classics ever written—along with the option to secure deluxe paperback, hardcover & box set editions at printing cost. Together, we can spark a new global literary renaissance alongside our small, independent publishing house called "The Library of Alexandria."

Thousands of years ago, the Library of Alexandria stood as a beacon of knowledge—until it was lost to history. We aim to reignite that spirit of preservation and discovery right now, in the modern age—only this time, it's accessible to all, in every language and every format.

Picture a world where every timeless classic, novel, poem, or philosophical treatise is not only available to read but also updated for today's readers—modernized, translated into any language or dialect, and ready to enjoy in any format you choose, whether that is in an eBook, audiobook, paperback, or deluxe hardcover & box set version a printing cost.

By joining our movement to rebuild the modern Library of Alexandria, you become part of an unprecedented mission to offer:

Unlimited Audiobook & eBook Access to the Greatest Classics of All Time

Instantly explore thousands of legendary works, from Plato and Shakespeare to Jane Austen and Leo Tolstoy. All are instantly ready to read or listen to, giving you a complete literary universe at your fingertips.

Paperback & Deluxe Editions at Printing Costs:

Purchase any title in a paperback, deluxe hardbound, or deluxe boxset edition at printing costs, shipped right to your doorstep. Curate your personal library of Alexandria with editions worthy of display— crafted to last, designed to captivate, and delivered straight to your door.

Modern translations for Contemporary Readers in all languages and dialects

Discover a vast selection of classics reimagined in clear, current language—no more struggling with outdated phrases or obscure references. Next to the original versions, we aim to offer translations in as many languages and dialects as possible.

As we continue our translation efforts and add new languages, readers everywhere can connect with these works as if they were written today. By bridging linguistic divides, you're contributing to ensuring that these timeless stories become more meaningful, accessible, and inspiring for people across the globe.

Your Personal Library of Alexandria:

Over the months and years, you'll curate a unique physical archive of classics—each volume a testament to your taste, curiosity, and love of knowledge. It's not just about owning books—it's about curating a cultural legacy you'll cherish and pass down for generations to come.

Join a Global Literary Renaissance:

Your support fuels an ongoing mission: allowing us to reinvest in offering deluxe print editions (including special boxsets) at their true cost, broaden the range of available formats and translations, and extend the reach of these works to new audiences worldwide. By joining today, you're not just preserving a legacy of masterpieces; you set in motion a powerful wave of literary accessibility.

We are more than a publisher—we're a movement, and we can't do it alone. Your support lets us scale our mission, preserving and reimagining history's greatest works for tomorrow's readers.

Become a Torchbearer of knowledge.

Thank you for picking up this book and allowing us into your literary journey. As you turn the pages, know that you're part of something larger: a global effort to keep these stories alive, share their wisdom across borders and generations, and spark a true cultural revival for the modern era.

If this resonates with you—please consider taking the next step by visiting:

www.libraryofalexandria.com

With gratitude and a shared love of knowledge,

The Modern Library of Alexandria Team

Visit:

www.libraryofalexandria.com

Or scan the code below: